ONCE UPON A TIME IN THE BLACK WEST

Dr. Robert H. Miller

Narrated by the Old Cowboy

ABOUT THE BOOK

The exciting adventures that slipped through the pages of history about Black Cowboys, Pioneers, Soldiers and Mountain Men are resurrected in *Once Upon a Time in the Black West,* a collection of beautifully woven short stories authored by *Dr. Robert H. Miller.* When you read along with the Old Cowboy narrating his adventures with his trusty canine companion Sundown, you'll be drawn back into a different place and era.

When the Old Cowboy speaks in a jargon that reflects his western heritage, you'll root for the likes of Nat Love. At the tender age of fifteen in 1869, he rode into Dodge City Kansas in its heyday and was enamored at his first glimpse of cowboys and decided he wouldn't be anything in life other than this. Again, there is an interesting story about how a young man of nineteen, half Cherokee-Indian and half African-American turned to a life of crimes. He watched his Native American family gets swallowed up by America's expansion into the West. After attending the Carlisle School for Indians in Pennsylvania, young Crawford changed his name to "Cherokee Bill." And the last story in this enthralling volume, the legend of "stagecoach" Mary Fields. After growing up on a plantation with her childhood friend, they reconnected thirty years later and she got Mary a job as a stagecoach driver carrying the United States mail. This is the first volume of many more thrilling stories to come in *Once Upon a Time in the Black West.*

***

The saga of the old West can't be complete until the full story is told. Once Upon a Time in the Black West is an effort to complete that saga and reinstate the lost pages of American history.

--Dr. Robert H. Miller

Table of Contents

"When Paths Cross"
How the Old Cowboy Met Sundown

Chapter One

They say hard times define a man. I say hard times can define almost anything. That's my opinion based on circumstances that led me to cross paths with a mongrel dog more courageous than 100 buffalos combined.

***

It was in Montana, I was plain out of water and my luck had run out. My horse had been shot out from under me and after walking for days, I'd lost any hope things would change. The sun treated me like a sworn enemy; it beamed down hard, sucking up what little strength I had left. I crawled like a dazed spider in the direction of big rock that offered me some shade.

Breathing like a runaway mustang, trying to dodge those angry heat waves, I made it to the rock. I checked my six guns... ouch! Just one bullet left. Times like these can make a man retrace his steps to figure out and question his own existence and what he had done to deserve such fate.

I have always prided myself in never losing sight of my surrounding, regardless of surrounding situations, but a few days ago, after leaving a lodge meeting with a few friendly Cheyenne Indians, for the very first time, I let my guard down. We had a friendly meeting and I said my good-byes but not before the Chief warned me to be on the look for a small band of Comanche on the war path.

From what he told me, some U.S. Cavalry soldiers raided one of their villages, killed a few women and children and stole some animal pelts. The Comanche wanted revenge. I assured the Chief that the Comanche and myself were on good terms. I'd be fine, I replied thusly.

Chapter Two

After two days in the saddle, I couldn't wait to get to the next town and get a hot bath and a good meal. My horse was also anxious to lay down on a soft bed of hey and get some needed rest. Perhaps we were both daydreaming. From a distance, I saw about seven or eight Indians riding toward us. I couldn't tell who they were but judging from the amount of dust accompanying them and the mean-sounding yell coming from their mouths, they didn't look friendly. When I saw the war paint on their faces, my conversation with the Chief flashed, faster than a squirrel could blink. I turned my horse around and like a jack rabbit running from a hungry coyote, we high- tailed in the opposite direction.

Arrows and bullets whizzed by my head as I galloped across the plains looking for shelter. They were gaining on me but my horse kept his steady pace, when I saw a hill, I figured if I could make it if I could defend myself. Turning my horse in that direction, I slapped the reins hard on his back. As we got closer to what looked like safe haven, a shot rang out and a carefully aimed bullet hit my horse and took him down.

Scrambling like wild geese in flight, I made it to the clump of rocks, but all I had was my six shooters. My horse lay dead on the ground as the Indians took my saddle, canteen, rifle, and everything else. All I could do was watch and hope they didn't come after me. With only four bullets to my name, I wouldn't last long. The war paint colors told me they were Comanche. Angry and ready for blood, anybody's blood but mainly the white men that murdered their families. I understood their angst and quest for vengeance; I just didn't want to die that day.

Chapter Three

Here I was, after another three days without food or water, in the shade of a rock with only one bullet left. Dying of thirst and trying to keep my mind together, I heard what sounded like a growl. When your body and mind get tired in the wilderness, you sure can begin to imagine weird things. Blowing wind can sound like a howling wolf, a swarm of bees or anything horrible. I heard the sound again, this time it was louder and I knew what it was. It was clear now. When I turned my head in its direction, the size of this animal at first glance looked like a big wolf. His growl was louder and more horrific now as he moved closer to me. Oh, dear! A mongrel dog. A piece of his left ear was torn off, he obviously had been in a fight. He limped a bit and his chest was scratched and covered in dried blood. He was a warrior.

I'd been around wild animals all my life, broke wild stallions, road buffalos bare back. I relied on that experience when I called out to him.

"Come here, boy!" I shouted.

He crouched down and growled louder, then showed his teeth. Something was wrong, this mongrel looked right through me as if he could see something on the other side. My instincts kicked in again and I turned my head slightly to the right. What I saw then, took my breath away.

When I turned back and faced the mongrel, we connected. I can't explain how but it's like we instantly knew what to do. I hit the ground faster than a sack of rocks; he jumped over me and landed on top of the biggest mountain lion I'd ever seen. Show time!

Those two animals spun around each other like a tornado on the plains of Missouri: biting and snapping at each other. I've seen wild stallions and big bear fight, but a mongrel dog up against a mountain lion... never! They laid into each other like a lightning bolt striking a water melon. At one point the scrappy canine had that big cat pinned to the ground, but the crafty lion simply rolled out from under him and sunk his teeth deep into neck of the brave dog.

The fight went on for a long while. It was intense and fierce. Then the mountain lion began to slowly subdue the dog. It became clear to me the mountain lion was going to win this battle.

Like a blind man searching for his cane, I clawed the ground around me looking for my gun. It must have fallen out when I dove to the ground. If I didn't find it soon, it would be all over for the dog, then I would next. When I looked up, the beat-up mongrel was fighting for all he was worth, his stubborn heart wouldn't let him quit. With his head hanging down, taking his last few breaths in pain, he gnarled and growled one more time. The mountain lion just looked at him and licked his chops. He was sizing the dog up for the kill.

Chapter Four

My aching right hand found my gun. With only one bullet left, I aimed carefully...one blink before that mountain lion leaped, I pulled the trigger and hit him right on the forehead.

With his tongue hanging to the ground, the mongrel limped over to me and lay at my feet.

"You 'bout the flightiest dog I've ever seen. Let me look at that leg," I said.

Later that day, we ate together. It's funny and strange how caring about somebody else can take your mind off your own pain. After our meal, my strength returned and so did his. We bonded that day, he saved my life and I saved his. Somebody was looking out for both us.

"Now, what am I going to call you big fella?" I said.

He just looked up at me and yawned. I racked my brain trying to come up with a name that suited this fine and brave animal but nothing seemed to fit. I scratched my head and looked across the plains and saw how beautiful the sun looked settling down behind the mountain tops. I laughed out loud.

"That's your name," I said.

By now he had wondered off a bit.

"Sundown, Sundown. Come on back here boy !!!"

He barked and ran back to me, wagging his tail. It was almost like he was waiting for me to come up with the right name.

Ever since the day our paths crossed, we've never left each other and never will.

The End

The Story of Nat Love

Chapter One

Sundown the West back in the old days was something to see. Covered wagons lined the plains like stars in a summer night sky. But there was one group of people who didn't like what they saw, the Indians. Watching all these new arrivals come in and make claims to their land was hard to take and it wasn't long before fights broke out between them and the white settlers.

The Indians didn't have a problem sharing their land, there was more than enough for everybody but the white man had other plans. He wanted it all for himself. He wanted to dominate over the native owners of the land. And that was the beginning of the strife.

One black man seeking to make his mark out West wound up having quite an adventure in Indian Territory. His name was Nat Love.

When Nat left the south at 15, he followed his instincts and headed West quicker than a bobcat returning to the wild. He arrived in Kansas full of smoke and fire with more courage than men twice his age.

In 1869, Nat rode into Dodge City Kansas like he owned it. He took to Dodge City like a thirsty man takes to water. He wanted to drink his fill and look for more. Dodge City was a wild town back then and everywhere he looked, there were cowboys; sitting in silver saddles on the back of big prancing horses, decked out in their finest clothes and showing off to beat the band. He had never seen cowboys before until now. He was impressed and drawn to them. He immediately made up his mind to become one of them. Nat noticed a man leaning against a building reading a paper. "Where can a man find work around here?" Nat asked. The man looked up and sized Nat up. "If you are looking for ranch work sonny, it's the Melody Saloon. Right over there" he pointed. Nat turned his horse in that direction and trotted over to the Melody Saloon. He'd been watching how cowboys carry themselves so he put on his best cowboy act, dismounted and walked into the Melody Saloon.

Nobody seemed to pay the young man any attention, it was full of cowboys and the music was loud and the cigar smoke was so thick it could blind an owl. He figured if he was gonna find work, the bar would be a good place to start. He decided to approach the meanest looking stranger at the bar. "Pardon me, stranger. Where can a man find work around here?" Nat asked. The man gave a weird stare at Nat and turned away. Young Nat wouldn't let me go anywhere until he answered him. So, he tapped the man on the shoulder. "Where can a man find work around here?" He asked again. The bar suddenly became enveloped in silence.

The stranger turned and faced Nat. "Don't you ever put your hands on me again sonny or I'll kill ya", he said. By now the cowboys in the bar all stopped what they were doing. The gambling tables got as quite as mice in a church. All eyes were on Nat.

As stubborn as ten Georgia mules, Nat showed no fear. He stepped back slowly, eyes steady on the stranger. "I'm just looking for work mister, what are you looking for?" Nat said. After staring at Nat for a minute, the stranger allowed a smile to creep across his face. He turned to the bartender. "Give this boy a drink on me." He turned back to Nat. "There's a Texas outfit camped outside of town. Be there at 6 in the morning. I hear they're hiring". Nat tipped his hat and left the bar. When he mounted his horse, he had a huge smile on his face.

On his way to the campsite that morning Nat became nervous. If he didn't play his cards right, his chance of becoming a cowboy would slip away. When he reached the campsite, the Boss was still having breakfast. He asked Nat to join him. Nat tried to look relax and he declined the gesture. While the Boss ate, he glanced up at Nat to size him up. With all that talent in Dodge City, he'd be taking a chance hiring a young boy with no experience. When the Boss finished he and Nat headed over to where they kept the wild horses. "You ever been on one of these, young fella?" He asked Nat. Nat thought carefully before he let out an answer: "Yes Sir!" Nat said. The Boss looked at Nat and smiled. "We'll see. "Bring out Good Eye", he shouted to Three of his men. It took three cowboys to bring out Good Eye, one of the wildest horses in the campsite. No cowboy there could stay on his back for more than three seconds before they were thrown off. Some of the best had tried and they all failed. "If you can ride him young fella then you got the job", the Boss said. Nat knew he had only one chance to prove he was a cowboy material. One of the cowboys that brought Good Eye over to him, whispered in Nat's ear. "He likes to go left, ride him to the right." They named this horse Good Eye, 'cause he was half blind. It took two men to keep that horse still enough to get a saddle on him. And finally, Nat's moment arrived. With all the courage he could muster, he climbed up on Good Eye's back and shouted: "Let him Go!!"

Like lightening shot out of a bottle, that horse leaped up in the air, twisted his neck left and right, then bucked three times. When his feet hit the ground, Nat was still on his back. Good Eye ran lackaday-split around the campsite like a spell was on him , tossing his head high in the air and bucking with his head tucked between his front legs, whinnying like a wild banshee, but Nat was still on his back. The other cowboys stood dazed and amazed at what they saw. Their mouths were left agape for so long, flies began to circle their heads. "Ride him young fella...ride him!!" They all chorused. They watched Nat do something none of them could do: staying on the back of Good Eye. Nat finally trotted Good Eye over to the Trail Boss and dismounted. "He's all yours, Sir. I'm done with him", said Nat with an air of confidence. The Trail Boss just looked at Nat. 'I ain't seen anyone ridin' like that in a long time. What'd you say your name was, son?" "Nat Love, Sir", he answered. "You got the job. We move out tonight." They shook hands, and that was the beginning for Nat Love: an American Cowboy.

Throughout the years, Nat's reputation for roping, riding and shooting spread like a wild fire, from Texas to Arizona, Nebraska and Mexico. All bets were on that he was the best cowboy in the Western Cattle country. But there were a few folks who thought otherwise. It was July 4th 1876 in Deadwood City, South Dakota where Nat proved, when it came to being a cowboy, nobody could out cowboy him. But before I tell you about that story, I can't help but talk about an incident on a cattle drive that could have ended young Nat's life and his reputation as the best man ever to break a wild horse and rope a steer.

Nat soon left Texas and joined up with Pete Gallinger's outfit. He was moving a large herd of cattle down along the Rio Grande. Nat's job was to deliver a herd up north, hundreds of miles from Mexico to Wyoming. That meant traveling through Texas Indian Territory, Kansas, Nebraska and the Shoshone Mountains, more Indian territories. The Apache, Comanche and Black Foot didn't take kindly to cowboys driving all those cattle through their land without paying them something in return.

Chapter Two

When cowboys didn't want to oblige them, the Indians just took what they thought was fair. Nat usually worked things out with them, maybe because of his color. The Indians generally respected the black cowboys because many of them were part Indians and could speak their language. Nat finally got his cattle to a place where the grass was short. That way whoever got guard duty could see anything that moved from a distance. One particular morning, as Nat stood watching, he noticed the cattle were little restless. "They're acting a little strange this morning," Nat said to one on the cowboys. "Something's got them riled up. Get back there," the cowboy shouted steer. Nat quickly dismounted and put his ear to the ground. Now he heard what the cows sense.

He got back up on his horse and shouted to his men. "Stampede! Buffalo Stampede! Nat hollered while circling the herd. He knew the only way to save them was to turn the buffalo in the opposite direction, that meant riding straight at 'em. He reared up on his horse so every cowboy could see him, fired his gun in the air and like a bullet shot from a Colt 45, all seventy men followed Nat's lead and charged straight at the stampeding buffalo.

With guns blazing, Nat and his cowboys galloped like bats out of hell, whopping and shouting, trying to do anything to spook the runaway buffalo in a direction away from the cattle.

The closer they came, Nat noticed one of his men was having trouble controlling his horse. When they got nearer, the buffalo split up into two. Unfortunately, one half cut right in the direction of the cowboy struggling with his horse. One thing about a bunch of runaway buffalo they know one direction only: straight ahead. When Nat looked over to check on his friend, the last thing he saw was the horse and the cowboy cut down under the hooves of two hundred runaway buffalo. By the time he got over to help it was too late.

By mid-morning, Nat and his men had recovered nearly all of the scattered cattle. What was left of the fallen cowboy was given a proper burial. Every cowboy knew his life could be snuffed out by an Indian's arrow, a gunfight over a woman, or an accident like a buffalo stampede. The only thing is, none of them ever wished to experience such.

Back to the event that happened on 4th of July in Deadwood City, South Dakota, 1876. Like I said, word was buzzing around town that Nat might not be the best shot or rider in the western territory. Big money was on Powder Horn Bill and Stormy Jim. That wasn't all, over 200 cowboys filled the town and they all thought they had something to say about it. I guess you could say, we had ourselves an old fashion Showdown! When the trail bosses and gamblers finished talking, they decided the first contest would be combine roping, breaking and riding a wild horse, all at the same time.

No telling where Nat was, by the time he signed up for the contest he was almost too late. Once the local sheriff explained the rules all those entered in the first event agreed. They all had to rope, bridle, saddle and mount a mustang in the shortest time. Nat smiled and anticipated a fun ride. He was legendary when it came to roping, riding and breaking horses. A trail boss from Dodge City waited until Nat's name was called, and then he slipped into the corral where they kept the wild mustangs. "Is Glass Eye ready"? He asked one of the handlers. "You bet, not even Nat Love can ride this killer, "he said.

Nat had a chance to look over the mustangs and was satisfied he could handle them. "Number 35. You're up!" The Sheriff announced. Nat hurried over to the corral ready to draw his horse when he heard another announcement. "I'm sorry to announce, there has been a change. Nat Love will be riding Glass Eye." A hush came over the crowd. Nat tried to hide his anger, but you could see he was piping hot. "Are you ready, Mr. Love?" Said the sheriff with an ounce of mischief. After a few moments of internal reflection, Nat tipped his hat signaling he was ready. The Sherriff fired his gun in the air and Nat shot after that mustang like a wolverine after a weasel. It was something to see.

He roped, saddled and bridled and mounted that wild horse in record time. Funny thing, Glass Eye must have remembered the first time he met this cowboy, he didn't give Nat any trouble at all. Nat won this contest, hands down.

The next contest was a bit trickier. This contest decided who would wear the title of the best shot in the western territory. The other legendary cowboy in the bunch doing a lot of bragging he would walk away with the title was none other than Stormy Jim. Nat had seen him shot in Amarillo once. Jim was the best he'd seen around. Maybe better than him. Maybe. He was entirely sure. Nat was counting on that. Once the trials were over to see who would face off, it came down to two men: Stormy Jim and Nat Love.

The judges decided each man would first shoot with a rifle then a Colt '45. Man with the most bullets in the bull's eye, rifle or Colt was the winner. The first round would be with a rifle. The Sherriff marked off 250 yards for the rifle contest, and 150 yards for the Colt 45, and then he flipped a coin to see who'd go first. Stormy Jim won the toss.

19

Jim was a tall slim man in his late 20's, stood as straight as a Comanche's arrow. He measured the distance and without taking his eyes off the target, lifted his rifle in one slick movement and fired ten shots. Eight bullets hit the bull's eye. The crowd went wild. That was some good shootin'. When the crowd simmered down, Jim waited for the sheriff's signal again, and drew his pistols, five bullets hit the bull's eye and five landed just outside. This time he was cheered with an ovation.

It was Nat's turn. The crowd had hushed down. Everybody wanted to see if this young cowboy could live up to his reputation. Nat approached the line and studied his target. He slowly picked up his rifle and caught everybody by surprise. At the signal, he fired from his hip and placed all 14 bullets in the bull's eye. It left everyone in utter shock. It was simply incredible!

He laid his rifle down and faced his other target. He waited for the signal, drew his Colt '45s and placed all ten bullets in the bull's eye. Stormy Jim couldn't believe it. He went up and checked the targets himself and there they were ten holes all in the bull's eye. This time the crowd tore out their voices and cheered louder than bunch of screaming eagles.

From that day on, Nat Love became known as Deadwood Dick, Champion Roper and Best Shot of the Western Cattle country. When he left Deadwood City, Nat rode out with his head up in the sky.

The Story of Cherokee Bill

Chapter One

Sundown. When the Old West was growing, opportunities to start a new life was open to everybody. All kinds of people came running: some good and some not so good. Some were looking for adventure; others were simply curious. Most of the people who did go running out there were looking to make dreams become a reality. Then there were the other kinds, the outlaws. To them an opportunity was anything that belongs to somebody else. They had a fast draw and were generally bad tempered. I knew a young fella like that but there was more to his story than most people know. His name was Cherokee Bill.

***

Crawford Goldsby was born around 1876, at Fort Conchos Texas. His father George was a sergeant in the 10th Cavalry and his mother Ellen Beck was a hard working God-fearing woman. His parents were of mixed blood. Part African-American and Cherokee Indian.

The family was upstanding and well respected. Little Crawford's family raised him to be an obedient son. Mr. Crawford was a busy man. His cavalry unit was all black and they had distinguished themselves so in battle, the Indians called them, the Buffalo Soldiers.

They were the Army's bravest and well trained fighting men this country has ever known. Despite their brave service, the 10th Cav. never received the respect they deserved from people in the white towns and ranchers they fought to protect or from the white soldiers they rescued many times, in the heat of battle.

Little Crawford learned about the sting of racial discrimination early on. He listened intently as his father talked to his mother about the unfair treatment he and his soldiers have to tolerate at Fort Conchos, and he could tell by the sound of his father's voice when he got angry. Lately that was happening a lot. One night at the dinner table, sergeant Goldsby let it all out:

"I'm sick of this!" He said to his wife.

"I told that Lt. We were riding into a trap. He didn't believe, and sure as hell Comanche's came from everywhere. We barely got out alive!" He said with disgust running through his voice.

Ellen Goldsby saw something in her husband's eyes that frightened her. She tried to calm him down, but she couldn't reach him. Little Crawford watched his parents talk, he noticed a look on his mother's face as she listened to her husband angrily retell the near death experience.

Later that night young Crawford approached his father sitting on the front porch. He was smoking his favorite pipe.

"We are still going fishing tomorrow, papa?" He asked.

George looked at his son and with a faint smile, replied:

"We ride out first thing in the morning son. But when I get back...we'll surely go fishing."

The morning after his father left, his son was awakened by voices in the next room. His mother was arguing with some man. Quietly he moved to the door of his room and peeked out.

"I said he ain't here and I haven't seen him since yesterday morning", his mother shouted.

"You must know where he is. He hasn't been seen nor heard from all day. Where is he hiding? The angry White Lt. asked.

Little Crawford could sense something bad was about to happen. Breaking into the room he pushed the Lt. away from his mother. Mrs. Goldsby demanded to know why they were looking for her husband. The Lt.'s story was, George got into some argument with some white folks in town. He and some the other black soldiers were defending themselves and things got out of hand and a white man was shot. The white folks said George did it and that was it.

"If he comes back here, he goes straight to jail" said the Lt. Mrs. Goldsby remained defiant. "Whatever my husband did, I'm sure he was right!" She said.

Young Crawford watched his mother try and hold back the tears. She didn't want to be weak in front him, especially now, when the Lt. Left the house, she cried out her husband's name, more in fear for his safety than for hers.

Chapter Two

Crawford never did go fishing with his father. It was some years later before he finally learned what happened to his daddy. Crawford's mother saw her son was growing up pretty fast. She also knew he needed to learn how to read and write but most of all, he needed to learn about his Cherokee background. So she sent him off to Cherokee Indian school.

The school was a big change for young Crawford, never before had he been surrounded by Cherokee Indians. His first day in class he heard stories about his people told to him in the Cherokee language. He learned how his people fought off white soldiers and settlers who tried to claim their land. The more he learned the truth about the Cherokee nation, the prouder he felt. He came from a people of noble fighters not cowards. Pride in himself and his people started busting out all over him like cherry blossoms in Spring. By the time he left that school, Crawford Goldsby had changed his name to Cherokee Bill.

When he got to the Carlisle school for Indians in Pennsylvania to get a more formal education, young Bill stood six feet tall. For a young boy in his early teens, he looked much older. After some time at his new school, he began to miss his family. He decided it was time to go home.

Returning home after 3 years, bill had all the makings of a good-looking young boy. He rode up to Fort Conchos stylishly dressed, with his hair blowing in the wind. Faster than water dancing on a hot griddle, Bill dismounted and ran to the sergeants' headquarters.

"Can I help you young man"? Asked the black sergeant. Out of breath Bill told him he was looking for his mother, Ellen Goldsby. The sergeant remembered the name.

"You are George Goldsby's boy?"

"You know my father?" Bill said with a brightened face. The sergeant told him he heard of his daddy and how the Army was trying to set him up to take the fall for some white settlers who started a ruckus with some black soldiers and few white settlers got killed.

"If my daddy killed anybody, they had it coming!" Bill said.

The sergeant told him he'd served with his father and that he was one of the bravest men he'd ever known. When Bill inquired about his mother the sergeant pulled some files and told him she had moved on to a Cherokee Indian reservation in Kansas. Bill knew exactly where that was. He mounted up and shot out of Fort Conchos.

Riding into Cherokee reservation back then wasn't a pleasant experience for young Bill. He saw his people all rounded up, living like bees in a honeycomb. His mind reflected on the stories he heard in school, how the Cherokee roamed all over this great land, fishing and hunting and living as one with God's green earth. Seeing his people living on handouts from the Federal Government to feed them, a government that didn't give a damn if a red or a black, man lived or died. This made him angry.

As he slowly rode through the area, he'd ask if anybody knew his mother, until an old Cherokee Indian woman pointed to a cabin down the road. Young bill's heart skipped more beats than a smooth stone thrown across a pond. When he got there, he dismounted and slowly walked to the

26

door and knocked. A man's voice, one he didn't recognize answered from inside:

"Who is it?" Bill answered, giving his old name.

"William Goldsby, Ellen's son."

The door slowly opened and there stood his mother. Bill remembered her as a pretty woman when he left, she looked much older now and frail. They hugged and cried. When they let go of each other Ellen stood back and admired her son. He was tall like his father and a pleasure to look at.

"You gonna stand there all day woman? I'm hungry, get me some dinner!" Demanded the man in the room.

"This is my oldest, William. I told you about him" his mother said.

The man looked at young Bill who stood over him.

"I'm Dunbar." He said.

He hated him at that instance but he knew his mother and younger brother had to put up with this fella after he left, so he bit his tongue and kept his cool.

"Nice to meet you, Dunbar" said Bill when he extended his hand.

Dunbar didn't even look at him, he just turned away and demanded Ellen to fix him his dinner.

After dinner Bill asked about his younger brother Clarence. His mother hesitated a bit then told him Clarence and Dunbar didn't get along so he moved out. Bill wasn't happy to hear that his family was already split up now Clarence was gone. When he looked around, he didn't like anything about the reservation or the way his mother was living there. The anger in him began to rise like a roaring sea. With every inch it rose so did his bitterness toward everyone and everything, especially white folks. Bill stayed over for a couple of days but he couldn't tell Dunbar wanted him out. He bode his mother farewell and mounted his horse and rode out of the reservation, never to look back again. As he rode off he knew he wanted something better for himself but the question of what, wasn't easy to answer.

Chapter Three

For the next eight years throughout Indian territory, Bill worked all kinds of jobs but his most preferred was working as a scout for the Cherokee, Creek and Seminole nations. He learned more about his people and the country they loved and the bitter feeling they had as white settlers with the backing of the Federal Government, took more and more of their land refusing to share it with them. By 1894, Cherokee Bill had grown into a young man of eighteen standing six feet tall, with long black hair hanging on his shoulder. He was armed with a quick smile and loaded down with saddle bags full of charm. While working as a scout he had mastered the art of using a six gun. Now he could draw and fire faster than you could blink an eye. The question now is, what would he do with all this talent?

Word had it that Cherokee Bill's life of crime started over a fist fight he got into one night in a dance hall somewhere. See, Bill was quite a ladies man, so they said. Another man by the name of Jake Lewis was also there and getting a little upset because his lady couldn't keep her eyes off Bill.

"Hey pretty boy, keep your smiles to yourself, you hear? Shouted Jake.

Bill being the kind of man he was, kept right on smiling, ignoring Jake. Jake finally had enough of Bill's playing around and challenged him to take it outside and settle it once and for all. Now Jake stood over six feet tall and rumbled around like a mountain with feet. But Bill wasn't one to back down.

The two men fought each other fist to fist and Jake beat the living day-lights out of Bill. He lay in the street with blood running all down his brand-new shirt, but what hurt him the most was his pride. Jake walked back into the dance hall feeling mighty proud of himself. He whipped that young pretty boy's behind and taught him a lesson he thought. Bill had gotten on his horse and rode out of town. Everybody thought he's had enough and ran like a coyote with his tail between his legs. They didn't know Cherokee Bill by a long shot. He came back. Kicking the dance hall door down, this time wearing his six iron.

"Jake Lewis, if you a real man come on outside, right now!" Bill shouted.

Jake looked at him and could see he was dressed.

"You sure you wanna die young boy?" said Jake with a smile on his face.

"Bring it out here", said Bill in a disdainful tone.

He backed out the door never taking his eyes off Jake. Once both men were outside, it was quiet for a split second. Then you heard more gunfire than on the 4th of July. When it was quiet again, Jake Lewis lay dead in the dirt with two bullet holes in his chest. No sooner had Jake hit the ground Bill was on his horse galloping out of town. Nobody had seen gunplay like that before.

Without taking his finger off the trigger, Bill used the palm of his other hand to make a fanning motion over the hammer of the gun causing bullets to fly everywhere. That's called "fanning": a style of gun play Bill invented. A lot of people tried to copy him later on, but nobody could do it as we as him.

Bill had committed his first crime and now a posse was hot on his trail. He needed a place to lay low for a while. Riding into a small town, he headed straight over to the saloon. In there he met up with a rowdy bunch of boys called the Cook brothers.

"So, what you running from boy?" Asked one of them.

Bill tried to act natural like everything was fine.

"You got on the run written all over your face. You kill somebody?" The other one asked.

Before Bill could say another word the door of the saloon blasted open. "It's marshal Ben Jackson and his men; they headed right this way!" Said one of the look outs. Quickly the Cook brothers downed their drinks and headed for the back door.

"You coming with us?" One of them asked.

Without thinking Bill grabbed his hat and off he went.

The marshal and his men were hot on their trail, but the Cook brothers had a hideout up in the hills. They got there just in time to set up and return gunfire.

"What's you name boy?" asked one of the brothers, but Bill was too busy returning fire. Taking his time, he aimed carefully and squeezed the trigger; and one of the marshal's men met his maker.

"Good shootin'. What did you say your name was?" Asked the other brother.

"Cherokee Bill."

Bill had killed his first lawman and a bounty was placed on his head. He and the Cook brothers went on a killing rampage so fierce they became number one on the most wanted list. Wanted posters decorated the territories like rice at a wedding. The reward money kept going higher and higher. Because Bill was so charming he always had a place to hide, the ladies helped him many times to escape the clutches of United States marshals and bounty hunters. He knew the Indian territories like the back of his hand. So, while white marshals and bounty hunters had to fear for their lives, Bill could ride through Indian unscathed.

Chapter Four

For two years Bill managed to avoid his pursuers until one day when the chase ended.

Bill's ex-girlfriend, Maggie Glass, invited him over for dinner one evening to meet her cousin, so she said. By now the reward money was over $1,500. That was a lot of money back then. Maggie had decided she loved the money more than Bill, besides they hadn't seen each other in a while. What Bill didn't know was the man she invited over was no kin of hers. The man was a US Marshal named Ike Rogers. Bill showed up decked out in his best clothes, you know, he wanted to impress her relative. When he got there he noticed Maggie was alone. He inquired about the whereabouts of her cousin and she gave the excuse he was running late and offered Bill a drink. He politely declined but chose to wait until her cousin arrived. Maybe it was something in the way Maggie moved and kept watching the window that worked Bill's instincts to a fever pitch.

"So, what does he do" asked Bill.

Maggie claimed she wasn't sure and poured herself a drink.

Sitting with his back to the door, it suddenly opened, and there stood Ike Rogers with a shoot gun in hand.

"Don't move or I'll blow you to kingdom come! Put your hands over your head!" Shouted Ike.

Starring coldly at Maggie who by now was counting the reward money, bill did exactly as he was told. Bill was a smart young fella, he knew the marshal was going to have a hard time keeping his shot gun trained on him and hand cuffing him at the same time. Rocking back on the legs of the chair, paying no attention the marshal's warning him to be still, Ike stepped forward to handcuff one of Bill's hands when Bill flipped the chair back and knocked him down. They fought like wild stallions, but Bill being the younger of the two, got the advantage. He wrestled Ike six shooter from his holster and was about to put a bullet in him when his lights went out. Maggie had knocked Bill in the head with a chunk of wood. When he came to, he was in a wagon, wearing leg irons and handcuffs on his way to jail.

Cherokee Bill's trial before Judge Parker at Fort Smith Arkansas was a major event. It seems as though Judge Parker also had a reputation, he was known as "hanging" Judge Parker. The courtroom was packed inside and out. Everybody wanted their last look at the famous, notorious, dashing young outlaw, Cherokee Bill. When he came before the Judge, Bill was loaded down in chains. Judge Parker was taking no chances. After Bill's lawyer finished making his case, the Judge calmly looked Bill in the face and sentenced him to hang by the neck until dead. Then slammed his gavel.

The hanging was scheduled for sunrise the next morning. One of the Cook Brothers who happened to be in the courtroom hollered out:

"Ain't no jail made can hold Cherokee Bill!" Bill's mother was there too. She pleaded with the Judge to show mercy. Judge Parker would have none of it. He knew Bill had killed innocent people and no mother's tears was gonna change his mind. He was also aware of Bill's escape record. Judge Parker gave strict orders, "no one was to speak to Bill in his cell."

Bill was helped down the steps to a jail underneath the court house. His mother followed close behind wiping the tears from her face. One of the prison guards stopped her.

"I'm sorry mam but you can't go no further." He said.

Bills mother pleaded with the prison guard to see her son just one more time before morning, when they would take him away forever. Now normally the guard would have stood his ground but he looked at Bill and perhaps thinking about his own son, he broke down.

"You better make it quick, the Judge will have my hide if he finds out about this." He whispered.

The prison guard allowed Bill's mother just a few more moments alone with her son. He'd wish he hadn't. When Bill's mother got close to his cell she slipped him a gun.

"Son, you ain't gonna hang like you father." She spoke with defiance.

Those words hit him in the chest harder than the kick of a Georgia mule. He never found out what happened to his father. Growing up he always figured his daddy got away and was hiding out somewhere.

"They hung papa?" Bill asked, his voice quivering with anger.

"You run you hear me. They ain't gonna hang my boy, run." She said.

The guard poked his head around the corner to see what was going on. Bill had hidden the gun in his shirt.

"Come on mam, you got to go now! Whispered the guard. Those were the last words to come from his mouth before Bill opened fire, killing him on the spot. Bill quickly grabbed the keys and unlocked the cell. Another guard came running down to check out the noise only to meet another bullet from Bill's gun. Now he was out in the street, running for a free horse, firing left and right. Gunfire from other guards rained down on him like a Texas hail storm but Bill was like a young deer, ducking, and zig-zagging, making them miss. He spotted a free horse and jumped on it and headed lackaday spit for the far end of town. Judge Parker took extra precautions that day, just in case something like this would happen. He had called in extra troops to make sure all exits and entrances to the town were heavily guarded. Galloping for all his worth, Bill soon realized he was boxed in, then the unexpected happened a bullet from a guards rifle shot the horse right out from under him. With Winchester rifles starring him in the face from every direction, he surrendered. It was over. Back to jail he went, this time for good.

Sunrise the next morning Bill was up and about carrying on like he was going to a picnic. The guards walked him out into a courtyard full of people. About 25 feet ahead stood the gallows. Judge Parker had allowed Bill's mother to walk with her handcuffed son, one last time. As Bill looked over a crowd of a 100 or more people he said,

"Looks like something gonna happen."

His mother watched her eldest son walk up the steps to the gallows whistling, acting like he couldn't wait to get it over with.

"Have you got anything you'd like to say?" asked Judge Parker.

"I didn't come here to make a speech...I came here to die!" Said Bill.

On March 17, 1896. Cherokee Bill, that is William Goldsby was hung until dead. But that's not the end of the story. They say his younger brother Clarence caught up with Ike Rogers and shot him dead. Nobody knows for sure what ever happened to Clarence after that. As for Maggie Glass, I don't know if she ever got the reward money, since Ike was

36

killed shortly after Bill's hanging. She just might not have collected a penny. You know, life's funny, given a different deal of the cards Cherokee Bill might have turned out better. I guess that's something we'll never know.

The End

The Story of
"STAGECOACH" MARY FIELDS

Chapter One

Sundown! Sundown!! Get on back here boy! What are you running after out there? You just want to chase some rabbits or something? Come on over here. That's a boy. Let me light my pipe. You know Sundown, the West in those early days was as untamed as a mustang stallion and some of the folks going out there were just as wild and full of vinegar as the land itself. Well, even a mustang can be tamed after a while, but it takes a mighty strong back and willful soul to do it. Mary Fields was one of those folks: stubborn and full of snuff.

****

As near as I can remember, Mary Fields was born in Hickman County, Tenn in 1832. Like most African-Americans born in this country at that time, Mary and her folks were slaves. They lived on a plantation owned by the Dunns.

"She's gonna be something someday, just see how she holds her head? " Her mother would say with a tinge of hope.

Even as a baby girl, Mary showed early signs of unusual strength for her age and had an independent streak bigger than the Rio Grande.

Picking cotton wasn't what Mary liked to do, but when her daddy talked about plowing the fields and hitching up the horses, he got her attention fast. Mary liked hitching up the plow horse; it gave her a chance to mount him and plow the fields with her daddy and have some fun all at the same time.

As a young girl, Mary often played with Dolly, the Dunns' daughter. With not much for a little white girl to do on a plantation, the two played together most of the time and became close friends. They were always getting into something. They were like a pack of raccoons on a holiday.

Their blooming friendship was a form of concern for Mary's mother as she knew the rules of the plantation. There would come a time when Dolly and Mary would have to part ways. The sad truth is that the white children could only play with slaves their age up to a point, then they were taken away to learn their place as the master or mistress of the plantation in order to rule over the slaves.

Mary's mother did try to explain this to her daughter but Mary wouldn't listen. As true as a hound's nose on the trail of a jack-rabbit, when Mary and Dolly grew up, Dolly left the plantation and Mary lost her best friend.

Chapter Two

Slavery thrived in the land for a long while; Blacks were treated as sub-humans, bought and sold. However, nothing that evil can last forever. Soon the North and South bumped heads over whether slavery should end or spread beyond the Mississippi. The Civil War settled the matter and by the time it ended, the South lost and that brought an end to slavery.

Up until the end of the Civil War, Mary had been a slave with the Dunns for nearly 30 years but with a new lease on life, she had the chance to leave but decided to stay. It was a much smaller plantation now, many of the slaves had moved on. When the Dunns figured they'd move to Ohio, Mary went right along with them.

Ohio seemed to be a fine place but Mary wasn't very happy there. She spent most of her life in Tennessee and a piece of it ended when she left. One day, while cleaning up around the place a letter post marked from out West arrived with her name on it. Since Mary could read and write, she excitedly open the letter. When she read the letter, her face lit up like a starry sky on a June night in Texas. Her childhood friend Dolly was now a nun. Sister Amadeus was how she signed the letter and she wanted Mary to join her at St. Peter's mission, 17miles from Cascade, Montana. Mary dropped everything and made preparations to join her friend. After spending 50 years with the Dunns, Mary packed her things and headed West.

Chapter Three

Many years had passed since sister Amadeus and Mary ran like chickens around the Dunn plantation in Tennessee, so you can imagine when Dolly, now a nun felt when opened the door and laid eyes on her best friend after over four decades. There stood Mary, standing 6' tall, wearing man's pants and jacket, a six shooter strapped low on her waist and smoking a cigar to boot! The sight must have been enough to choke a mule. They both were pleased as punch to see each other. After catching up on old times, Mary was ready for work.

The mission was old and needed repairing. Workers moved stones and were fixing whatever needed fixing. Mary fit right in, she was as strong as many of the men on site. She sometimes loaded the wagons by herself. It wasn't long before she became the head honcho of the crew. When Mary became their boss, the men took to cussing and moaning. Many of them were white and they didn't take kindly to having a black woman as head cowpuncher.

"...mind your own business, black Mary" shouted one of the men.

"I'll mind your business, and if you don't like it, we can take it to the street!" Mary roared back, with the cigar flapping in her mouth.

It was in July, a day so hot you could fry an egg on the palm of your hand. Mary was hauling stones for the mission. She had unloaded her wagon and, was feeling sassy, and started poking fun and meddling with the men. This one fella was new, but that didn't bother Mary any bit, she treated him just like the rest. "Okay, mister sack of lard, get a move on! We can pitch two stone shacks up here in the time you take for lunch", Mary said.

A few men laughed. They were used to her by now. This new fella didn't find it amusing.

"Since when does a black slave boss a white man?" He queried.

"Ain't no slaves here mister. Now I said get a move on it!" Mary shouted.

Wasn't no fun in her voice now. Mary was mad. The new guy was tired and out of sorts. He made a terrible mistake. He walked up to Mary and swung and knocked her square on her behind. Everybody stopped what they were doing. They were watching Mary like blackbirds in a cottonwood tree, wondering what she would do now. She was off the ground and on her feet faster than a hot knife through spring butter. Cigar still in her mouth, she dusted off her pants. In a fierce tone, Mary said:

"Strap on your guns mister and meet me in the street."

The workers all stunned, looked at each other as if they couldn't believe their ears. A black woman putting a challenge to a white man for a gunfight? Nobody in those parts ever heard of such a thing. They sure didn't know Mary fields. The West in those days had a code and this stranger knew it very well. If anybody, man, woman, or child put out a challenge, you had to take it up, or ride out of town. Seeing Mary was a black woman and he was a white man, if he backed down, he'd have to leave the territory. The stranger strapped on his gun and moved slowly into the street. When he reached the center, Mary was already waiting for him.

At midday, Mary cast a shadow that seemed to block out one whole side of the street. Standing about 20 paces away from the ornery stranger, she starred down on him... hard. Her face shone like the color of a burned prairie and the smoke from her cigar curled around her head like a rattlesnake ready to strike. Silence fell over the workers like a witch's spell. Mary stood her ground, waiting for the man to make his move. The fingers on the stranger's shooting hand twitched nervously. He ground the heel of his boot into the dirt as he figured his shot. Quicker than a squirrel can blink, he went for his six shooter but Mary was faster. She fired 3 shots to his one, and varmint keeled over into the dust, taking his last gander at the sun before knocking on heaven's door. Mary, still chewing on her cigar, walked over to the mission grounds triumphantly and started feeding the chickens.

"It was fair and square. No man lays a hand on me", Mary said to the workers.

After that, no man ever raised his hands in Mary's face.

Word of the gunfight got back to the Bishop in charge of the region. He felt Mary's reputation was causing more problems than the mission needed. After ten years of dedicated service, he demanded that Sister Amadeus fire Mary. The good Sister knew she couldn't change the Bishop's mind but she also knew she didn't want to part from her childhood friend either. That night she thought and prayed how to keep Mary at the mission, then an idea flashed through her mind.

Chapter Four

As luck would have it, a rumor had been circulating around town that the United States mail service was opening a new route between Cascade Montana and St. Peter's mission. The route would be tough. It followed a scrawny mountain trail that passed through the bad lands crawling with desperados and hostile Indians. Only the strongest and most experienced men even thought about taking the job.

"That's it! Exclaimed Sister Amadeus, "Mary will get that job."

The next morning, she explained to Mary about the mail delivery job.

"You don't have to take it if you don't want to. It could be very dangerous." She said.

But to Mary, there was something about the job that set right with her. I suspect the danger associated with it and the newness of the job and that no woman had ever done it before appealed her.

"If a man can do it, I can and if a man can't do, I still can.

Now who do I see about the job?" Mary asked.

Sister Amadeus told Mary the United States mail Depot Manger did the hiring. If she could impress him, she'd get the job.

There were at least 40 men standing around the Depot that day looking to be hired. They all turned at once in the direction of thundering hooves and a cloud of dust. Mary had arrived wearing buckskin pants, a man's jacket and a Stetson hat. She jumped off her chestnut brown stallion, and with a rifle in one hand, cigar chomped between her teeth, walked through the crowd of men like a rooster parading around a barnyard full of hens.

"I'm here for the driving job, who's the boss here?"

She had a way of talking, typical of an Army General leading his men into battle. From the Mail Depot came this little white fella looking to see what all the commotion was about.

" I'm doing the hiring, who wants to know?" He shouted.

Mary stepped right up and faced him square on.

"I'm here for the mail delivery job, where do I sign up? Mary asked.

The Depot Manager looked stunned.

"You're a woman, this job is for a man," He said.

He tried to walk around her but Mary blocked the doorway.

"You hiring drivers, ain't you? Well I'm a driver and a darn good one," she said. "I can drive six teams of horses better than any man here."

The Depot Manager was getting a little riled. He didn't expect a black woman to talk like this to him, especially in front of other white men. With his lips drawn tight across his teeth and his fists dug in on his hips, he said:

"If you can drive six teams of horses better than any man here, you got the job! But first you got to hitch them up.

They're over there," he pointed to the livery stable where they kept the horses.

Mary knew all the men were watching her, knowing she had an audience played right into her hands. She walked over to the livery stable and hitched those horses up so fast it would have made you dizzy just watching. Faster than you can giddy up, she had the horse reins in one hand and a bullwhip in the other.

"Move it! She shouted.

With one crack of that whip, those horses took off like they had been stung by a swarm of yellow jackets. Mary drove those horses around that yard in 10 different directions, yelling:

"Move it!"

Dust whirled around her head like a tornado. The crack of that whip made it sound like the 4th of July celebration. She brought the horses to full stop right in front of the Depot Manager. Smiling at the crowd of men, she teased,

" Can any of y'all do that?"

He hired her on the spot and that's how Mary Fields became the first black woman and some say the first woman to ever carry the United States mail. She was 60 years old when she got that job.

Chapter Five

For 8 years Mary delivered the mail from St. Peter's mission to Cascade, Montana and she always on time. One day, sister Amadeus had fallen sick, Mary had to travel a distance to get the special medicine she needed. On her way back, like a bullet shot from a Winchester rifle Mary, took every short cut she knew. She ran those horses faster than they had ever run, she took all they could give, and then some. Her wagon was also loaded down with dry goods. The mission's food supply was shorter than the eyelashes on a rattlesnake.

The thought of her childhood friend lying in bed sick drove Mary on. She didn't stop to rest, her mind was fixed on Sister Amadeus. Perhaps that was why as night began to fall, Mary was coming down over the top of a hill, she didn't see the dry gully below, when her wagon hit it, it sounded like thunder rolling across a dreary sky. Her freight was everywhere. Working faster and harder than ever before, she got nearly all her freight back on the wagon. By now darkness had crept in and she began to hear the howls of lingering wolves and coyotes. There was a full moon that night and Mary welcomed it like a thirsty man given a chilled cup of water. She clutched her trusted rifle. She didn't have time to build a fire before nightfall to keep the wolves and coyotes away. So there she set her finger on the trigger of her rifle when out of nowhere she heard a growl, coming from the left side of her wagon. Mary turned and fired three shots.

"Get back, all you rascals," she shouted, then fired three more times in different directions.

You could hear the wolves scampering away like a flock of geese. The echo from her rifle blast must have scared any other creatures from coming forth. She didn't have no more trouble that night. At day break Mary snapped the reins on her horses back sides and they were off again.

Sister Amadeus was still very sick but when she saw Mary break through the door with the medicine her spirits were lifted.

"Don't worry 'bout a thing, I'm here now...it's gonna be alright." Mary smiled.

Eight years is long time for a sixty year old woman to be hauling mail. She finally gave up the job and with the help of Sister Amadeus, opened up a laundry business in Cascade Montana. You'd thought by now she would have settled down, not at all! See, Mary used to do laundry on credit for the cowboys coming through town on cattle drives. While having a friendly drink in the towns saloon, she spotted a cowboy who owed her money. As he headed for the door, Mary followed him to make sure she had the right man.

"Hey you!" Mary shouted.

The cowboy turned around.

"You owe me for laundry...now pay up!"

He looked at her and started laughing.

"You got me mixed up with somebody else", and turned to walk away.

She spun him around and with one punch...dropped him to the ground. Mary planted her foot deep in his chest.

"Pay me my money"! The stunned cowboy reached in his pocket so fast he pulled out all the money he had. Mary grabbed it, counted out what he owed and threw the rest in his face and walked away.

***

On her 80th birthday Mary was laid to rest in Cascade Montana. Her childhood friend, Sister Amadeus had passed away a few years earlier while opening up another mission in Alaska. The people in Cascade Montana had taken to Mary like a young boy to stray pup. They buried her at the foot of a mountain trail that leads to a winding road heading for the St. Peter's mission. It was a road that she had traveled for many years, hauling freight and the US Mail for a mission and a nun, who was her childhood friend.

You know Sundown, Mary Fields had more courage than any man I know. Legend has it at night, when the winds blow down that mountain trail, you can hear the thundering hoof beats of Mary's horses, her whip cracking in the night air and loud voice saying, "Move it!"

The End

Made in the USA
Las Vegas, NV
03 October 2023

78523085R00038